It's All
In Your Mind

How a teen rewired her mind to
radically change herself,
her life and her family

by Lindy Lumbert

This book is dedicated
to the
one eye love

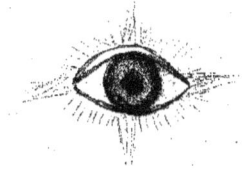

Blossom Books
ALTAMONTE SPRINGS, FL

Dear Diary,

 Today is my birthday.

 Dad gave me this diary then told me I could have anything I wanted.

 I got excited.

 "ANYTHING???????" I asked.

 "Within reason, of course," he answered.

 Oh sure. There's always a catch.

 'Within reason' leaves out everything I want.

 Including......

 a sister around my age

 a brother I'd like instead of the one I've got

 more special days with my grandmother that just died and a new face to go with the new hair that I'd ask for, too.

 a horse that I could keep in the back yard

 piano lessons, which means I'd also need a piano

 dance lessons that would make me graceful, which means I'd need new feet, too.

 Within reason.

 I know what kind of presents those are.

 The kind that look like they would make you happy, but then they don't.

 The kind that last only for a short while then leave you wanting for more.

 I just really wanted something more.

 Presents like Dad was thinking of are just things that come and go.

 New clothes go out of style. New albums get outdated. New games get boring.

I wish Dad could buy a magic wand that would magically transform me.

Now that would be a present.

I know. Not within reason, right?

I really can't think of anything he could give me that would make me like myself.

I'm smart enough to know that's what I really need.

I think I'll just keep this diary and ask for a blank check to be used when I know what to ask for.

I can treat this diary like my sister and my closest friend.

It can help replace my grandmother that is no longer here to confide in.

I can tell it things that I wouldn't tell anyone else.

I can share my hopes and dreams and wishes with It .

It will never judge me or tell me I can't be all the things I wish I was.

It can be my something lasting.

Dear Diary,

My brother gave me a birthday present this morning.
It was a cute little hair brush for my purse.

The card said

> For the Girl with the
> Oughtabeen Hair

How sweet, I thought. "But you spelled auburn
wrong."

"It's not auburn. It's oughtabeen."

When I looked puzzled long enough, he told me what
it meant.   "Ought-a-been on a dog!"

HOW RUDE.

I screamed at him, "George! You're giving me a complex!!!"

"No, that's a hairbrush. I didn't even know you
wanted a complex."

Ahhhh!!!!!

Why me????
Why did he have to be my brother?

Dear Diary,

This afternoon I went to the mall with Wendy. She's always fun to hang out with and we never run out of things to talk about.

Or should I say we never run out of boys to talk about.

That seems to be our favorite subject.

Anyway, I had such a good time that by the time I got home, I totally forgot about being angry with my brother..... at least until dinner.

At the dinner table, George handed me a gold box with tons of bows on it.

I asked him what it was.

He said it was what you thought I was giving you for your birthday - an inferiority complex.

"Very funny," I said and opened the box.

I looked at George in surprise!

"It's empty."

"Of course," he grinned. "It's a joke. Nobody can really give you a complex. That's something you have to give yourself."

Then my whole family laughed.

What's so funny about that???????????

I should have asked for a way to get George to stop bugging me.

Now THAT would be a present.

Dear Diary,

Nothing exciting happened today.

I had a boring morning.

I also had a boring afternoon.

I am writing this before dinner, but that's okay, because the way things are going, I'll have a boring evening, too.

boring
   boring
      boring
         boring
            boring
               boring
                  boring

Dear Diary,

Mother is going back to work.

She said she always intended to go back after she raised her kids. She said it's no big deal.

No big deal to her maybe.

I mean it's true I don't want her around all the time, but I still want her here when I want her here.

Oh, and this afternoon she's going to sit down and make a list of things she wants me to do around the house.

Mother said she gets bored just staying home alone and doing housework. She wants to spread her wings and have a little freedom.

I thought that's what kids got to do.

But now that she is going to work, I'll be the one bored and staying home alone doing housework.

She's always been here when I get home from school. Now I'll just come home to an empty house.

Of course George will be here, but that's about as good as being alone.

I take that back.

I think I'd rather be alone.

It sure sounds like I'm getting the worst end of this deal, doesn't it?????

Got to go now.

Mother is calling me. It must be time for that list.

A whole list! Can you imagine that?

I can't wait until I'm a mother so I can get my kids to do all the work while I go out and do what I want!

Dear Diary,

Remember that list I told you about???

Well, it's long. And I do mean lo-ong.

Mother said she heard me telling Wendy that I'll be bored when she starts working, so she added a few extra things to the list.

"Don't worry about being bored," she said. "Just do your chores with the radio on and time will fly."

I should have told her that if I wanted to see time fly, I'd throw a clock out the window.

Really though, sometimes I feel like the whole world is against me. First, I have to stay home and she doesn't.   Then I have this brother to deal with all by myself and then I get this long, long list. With a list like this, I may not get bored, but I won't have time for fun either.

I AM TIRED OF BEING TOLD WHAT TO DO!

My fun and happiness depend on everybody else. I am so tired of feeling miserable.

Why are we here anyway?

It seems like there must be a reason I don't know about, but whatever it is, I don't think my parents know either. They seem just as miserable in their world as I am in mine.

Sometimes I think maybe George knows.

I always thought that my life would be fine if I wasn't a kid.

I have doubts about that now.

Mother said she was going to work because she was bored. I guess that means you don't stop being bored just because you grow up.

Dear Diary,

 I AM SO HAPPY!

A new boy came to our school today and they put him in my class!

 His name is RODNEY and he is WONDERFUL!

 I think I'm in love.

 Ever since I saw him, I haven't been able to think of anything else.

 That's love - isn't it?

 The only thing I know is that when I look at Rodney, my old boyfriend doesn't interest me anymore. I guess that means I have a new boyfriend.

 It sure feels good to be in love.

 It will feel even better if I find out that he likes me back.

Rodney   Rodney

                              Rodney

              RODNEY

 Rodney

                              RODNEY

              Rodney

Dear Diary,

Because of Rodney, I had a terrific day at school. He smiled at me in home-room and I got goose bumps.

I didn't think of anything but him all day and I felt like I was walking on a cloud.

I WISH I COULD MAKE THAT FEELING LAST!

It only lasted until I got home though.

Once I saw my annoying list of Things To Do, I got really depressed.

It just seemed like too much work. I couldn't face it, so I just curled up on the sofa and started daydreaming about how great my life will be when I'm grown up and nobody can tell me what to do.

It will be so great!

If I don't want to do something, I won't.

And nobody will be making lists for me either!

I wish I could be an adult NOW!

Of course, I'd wish for Rodney to be an adult now too.

Rodney. Rodney.
He's my man.
If he can't do it....
Nobody can!

Dear Diary,

This is a very sad, sad world.

Remember Mother's idea of going to work so she could get out and do what she wanted to do?

Well, it looks like it backfired on her.

Tonight she was complaining about her boss, and then Dad chimed in and started complaining about his.

So adults have bosses too?

Why do you suppose Mother was so anxious to go to work? Does she like having someone tell her what to do?

I know I don't.

But I don't have a choice.   She does.

At least I thought she did.

I really thought that when I grew up nobody could tell me what to do.

What's the use of growing up?

Does it never get any better?

Mother even said that now she feels like she has 2 bosses to answer to - Dad and Mr. Caddy.

I wonder if she ever has time to answer to herself.

I can't imagine spending my entire life doing what somebody else tells me to do.

Something is wrong somewhere.

Who bosses the bosses?

Someone in the world must boss himself, and whoever that is ---

I'M GOING TO FIND HIM!

Dear Diary,

In social studies today, I was trying to read my text book, but the words just went right by me. They didn't sink in at all.

Suddenly I realized that I had read 3 pages, but I really couldn't tell you what I was reading about. My mind was on vacation.

My teacher noticed it before I did. She said I had a blank look on my face and asked me what I was reading about.

I couldn't even fake it........ I had no earthly idea.

She accused me of not knowing how to concentrate.

I really can though. It's just that I don't like to concentrate on the things that she wants me to.

I tried a concentration test just to be sure she wasn't right. I tried timing myself to see how long I could hold my attention on one subject.

It was easy really.

I just started daydreaming about Rodney and I didn't even want to think about anything else.

I did a great job and I would have lasted longer than 18 minutes, too, if that silly teacher hadn't broken my concentration.

I was so focused that it took me a minute to remember where I was.

Meanwhile the teacher's going on and on about how I'll never learn to concentrate.

I knew she wouldn't understand, so I just let her talk.

Dear Diary,

I'm s-o-o-o-o embarrassed. I can never go back to that school.

All I was doing was practicing my concentration, trying to break my 18 minute record, while my science teacher was doing some kind of weird experiment.

It's not that I didn't see him get out the two glasses. It's not that I didn't know he put water in one and alcohol in the other.

I was even watching when he put a worm in the water. The worm wiggled around a little and then climbed up the side of the glass.

Not very interesting though. Then Mr. Moss took the poor little worm off of that glass and dropped him in the alcohol.

I swear the worm just disintegrated right in front of our eyes. Disappeared! Gone!

That really did break my concentration.

BUT NOT SOON ENOUGH.

Mr. Moss asked me what the experiment proved.

Why me?????

Twenty -eight kids in the class and he had to pick on me!

OOOh, it was so hard. I was straining my brain, but I really hadn't been thinking about the experiment at all.

"What did this experiment prove?" Mr. Moss demanded. I just stared at him so he asked me again.

I just said the first thing that popped into my mind. "If you drink enough alcohol, you'll never have worms."

Wrong answer I guess.

The whole class started cracking up.

Well, everyone except Mr. Moss that is. He just shook his head and looked at me. "Young lady, your mind has not been with us at all lately. What DO you spend your time thinking about??

All the girls started to giggle and whisper. They knew exactly what I was thinking about and some of them even pointed to Rodney.

So now Rodney knows too.

He made like he didn't notice though and answered the question.

He said If alcohol will kill a worm, imagine what it does to you.

Right answer, I guess. Nobody laughed - especially me.

I think Rodney was just trying to let everybody know that he was concentrating on the experiment.

He obviously wasn't thinking about me!

I felt so incredibly embarrassed, I wanted to die.

I made a total fool out of myself and there was nowhere to hide.

Dear Diary,

George told my parents the worm story!

HOW DID HE FIND OUT????

Is it so funny that the whole school is talking about it?

Well, my parents obviously thought it was funny. They laughed themselves silly.

What's so funny about making one little mistake? I was really mad at George for making such a big deal out of answering one little question wrong.

He said that wasn't the funniest part. The funniest part was when I ran out of the classroom crying.

Now what is so funny about that?

AND WHO IS THE BIG MOUTH THAT TOLD GEORGE? I didn't even write you that part.

George says he can't believe I let it bother me so much when people laugh at me.

He acts as if I had a choice.

Now tell me the truth. Is there anyone who likes being laughed at?

That George.

Either he knows something I don't or he's just trying to aggravate me.

Knowing George, he's probably just trying to

Dear Diary,

Today is Sunday.

My parents are taking us to the County Fair. We'll probably be out late, so I won't be writing to you tonight.

Mother sounds like she's feeling a little guilty about going to work and leaving us alone after school. I think she's trying to make up for it by taking us out for the day.

Actually, it hasn't been a problem after all. We're doing fine alone and I almost enjoy doing the things on my list when I'm by myself.

It makes me feel pretty grown up.

I pretend that it's my house and that I thought of doing the work all by myself.

I even memorized the list so that I could throw it away. It really makes me feel important to accomplish something without being told what to do everyday.

Mother has nothing to feel guilty about.

But I'm not going to tell her that.

Dear Diary,

Why did God give me an older brother? What was he trying to tell Me? I thought God was supposed to love everybody. If so, then why did I get stuck in same family with good old George????

You won't believe what happened!!!!

While we were at the fair yesterday, he hurt my feelings AGAIN!

Everything was going alone just fine. We were all having a great time, then you-know-who decided we should all go on this humongous Ferris wheel.

I said I didn't want to go, but George wouldn't take no for an answer.

He kept teasing me and asking me why I wouldn't go on the Ferris wheel. Finally, I told him that heights scare me.

He went nuts. To him, that was ridiculous.

"Heights can't scare you," he said. "What do they do? Jump out and yell Boo?

"Heights don't even care about you. They just go on being high. The truth is, it's your own thoughts that scare you when you're in high places."

"What's the big hairy difference?" I yelled. Then he picked me up, threw me over his shoulder and carried me to that stupid Ferris wheel and plunked me down on the seat.

Everybody got in on the act. Dad ran over and gave the guy our tickets so he'd start the thing before I could get over George to get off.

I screamed the whole entire time!

To top it all off, they stopped the Ferris wheel while we were at the very top!

I was so-o-o scared. I was even crying. Then I started yelling at George for doing this to me. "George, I told you heights scare me. When will this thing stop???"

He looked me straight in the eye and said, "Whenever you want it to."

"Oh, sure," I whined. Does that mean somebody way down there will hear me if I yell GET ME OUT OF HERE!? Or is there a two-way radio up here that I don't know about?"

His answer - "Neither. When you decide that you don't want to be scared anymore, the feeling will stop. You can't control the Ferris wheel, but you can control how you feel."

That's the stupidest thing I ever heard. I told him it wasn't that I wanted to be scared. I can't help the way I feel.

All he said was, "wrong."

Then the Ferris wheel started moving again and I started screaming again.

We didn't talk about it anymore, but when we got off I told Dad that a girl should have the right to say when she didn't want to go on a ride.

Dad still thought the whole thing was very amusing.

Am I missing something here???

Dear Diary,

I can't get that conversation with George off my mind - that stuff about being able to control your feelings.

I'd sure like to believe stuff like that is true.

.....You know I've been wondering if George knew some kind of secret.

I mean there's got to be some reason he manages to be in a good mood most of the time.

Hardly anything bothers him.

And he does laugh a lot, even if it is at my expense.

Maybe he does know something.

At any rate, I'm going to find out.

I'm going to have a talk with George today.

I'm not sure what I'll say, but I'll figure that out when the time comes.

Dear Diary,

George won't tell me ANYTHING!

I really tried talking to him.

I told him I was tired of being bossed around and that everybody picks on me.

He got very quiet.

Then he said, "Close your eyes."

I closed them. I was ready to hear the magical answer that would change my entire life.

Then he said, "Now with your eyes closed, try to imagine...... how little I care."

Unfortunately I could imagine it and it hurt more than I could stand. I ran up to my room and cried like a baby for more than an hour.

I was still crying when Mother got home and she insisted on knowing what was going on. I told her what George said to me and she had a talk with him.

But she really didn't understand.

How could she?

She doesn't know George's secret either.

She doesn't even know he has one!

I wasn't crying because George hurt my feelings, but because he wouldn't tell me his secret so that I can be as happy as he is.

Dear Diary,

I had such a lousy day today.

Nothing really bad happened, but I'm still so disappointed about that secret.

I really did believe that I was going to hear the answers I've been looking for.

I am so tired of hurting so much and feeling so miserable.

I guess even you can't understand me this time. You don't even know what it's like to have feelings.

One minute I'm up. The next minute I'm down.

No wonder old people look so worn out.

Everything can be going along just fine, then ZAP, something bad happens.

Then you have to wait for something good to happen so you can feel okay again.

I can't imagine going on like this for 90 more years.

There has to be a better way!

Dear Diary,

Stephanie came and sat with Wendy and me at lunch today. She just got her hair cut and it really looked great.

When Stephanie sat down, Wendy said ,"Your hair looks beautiful today."

Stephanie answered, "It really does, doesn't it?"

I choked.

I couldn't believe Stephanie was so conceited.

I rolled my eyes at Wendy.

Wendy made a face and tried to look all innocent.

When Stephanie left, she told me that she didn't think that was conceited at all.

"What did you want her to do? Pretend she hates her new hairdo? Or that she can't tell it looks good?

"If a girl doesn't like the way she looks, how can she expect anyone else to like it?

If she doesn't like herself, how can she expect anyone else to like her?", Wendy asked.

How could I answer that?

I never thought of it that way before.

I've always been taught to think of others,

be nice to my brother,

love my neighbor,

respect my father and my mother,

but I swear - NOBODY ever told me to love MYSELF!

Actually, I think it would be easier to love everybody in the world than to love myself.

I don't even know how to do that.

Ahhhhhh!!!!!!! D!

I just want to scream!!!!!

Wendy is sick of me. My mother is sick of me.

And I'm sick of me.

Who knows who else is sick of me, too?

I mean, how could I ever guess I would get on other people's nerves just because I don't like myself?

Like tonight -

Wendy came over and fixed my hair. She handed me a mirror and said, "Look. You're beautimous!"

I looked.

I did not see beautimosity. I just saw me.

"You don't have to say that just to make me feel good," I told her.

My mother said the new hairdo made me look absolutely lovely.

"I have a mirror. I can see I'm not lovely. You're just saying that because you're my mother."

That's when Wendy came unglued. "Okay then. Your hair looks weird. It looks like you've been using a comb with buck teeth. Do you like that better??

"I'm so tired of listening to you put yourself down. Can't you ever just say 'thank you' when you get a compliment? Do you always have to be so negative?

"If you are so convinced you are ugly, maybe you are right. Why would I want an ugly person for a friend anyway?"

Then she left. And now she doesn't want to be friends anymore.

Did you hear that? She doesn't want to be friends anymore. What am I going to do???

Dear Diary,

I fixed my hair this morning the way Wendy fixed it yesterday.

I saw her before school and apologized for being so negative.

Wendy said, "Your hair looks good."

I said, "Thank you."

We both smiled.

Then I opened my mouth again and out fell the words, "I know it won't last though. You know how crazy my hair is."

Wendy threw her hands up in the air and screamed, "YOU DID IT AGAIN!" Then she stomped off and wouldn't talk to me for the rest of the day.

It was a mistake........I didn't mean to put myself down again, but when you've been doing something for so long, it really is hard to stop.

Not that I'm not going to try.....

It's just hard. That's all.

Dear Diary,

Wendy still won't talk to me.

I was in a really bad mood when I came home. George said I looked like I just lost my best friend. He asked if there was anything he could do to help.

"I thought you didn't care!"

He just stared at me. "Of course I care. If I can help, I want to, but I don't care to listen to you complain, especially about something you can't change or something that you don't intend to change."

"Wendy thinks I'm negative."

"Oh. And you don't?", George asked.

"Well, I didn't realize it! But now if I don't find a way to like myself, even Wendy won't like me anymore."

George offered to play coach and show me exactly how to learn to love (or at least like) myself. He said he'd even give me homework to do.

I'M SO EXCITED. George is finally going to share his secrets with me!

Look out world - here I come!

My first assignment is to make a list of all the things I like about myself and a list of the things I dislike.

I'm going to go do that right now.

Dear Diary,

Boy have I got a long list........my dislike list, that is.

I couldn't think of anything to put on my like list.

I kept telling myself that to put something on my like list was not conceited.

I kept telling myself that if a girl doesn't like herself, nobody else will either, but I still couldn't think of anything to put on my like list.

When George looked at my lists, he shook his head. I said, "I'm sorry."

He said, "Your list is sorry. You have to have enough likeable things about you so people will be willing to overlook the not-so-likeable ones.

"What I do, is think about the things people like about me and do those things more.

"When I like myself, it makes me sort of magnetic. People are drawn to me even if they can't figure out why."

"But that's the problem. I don't like myself," I reminded him.

"You have to have some redeeming qualities. I think you've had such a habit of criticizing yourself that you don't ever give yourself credit for doing anything right."

Then George told me there's an exercise I could do that would help.

He said, "Bend your right arm at the elbow and then reach your arm up and touch your back."

So I did and raised my eyebrows in question.

"Now tap 3 times."

Very funny.

 He just made me pat myself on the back.

Very funny. Very, very funny.

"It really works," he said. "It's not a joke. Every time you realize you did something right, pat yourself on the back and very soon you'll have things to put on your like list."

Dear Diary,

Hey. I actually got my first opportunity to pat myself on the back.

Mallie saw the A+ on my math test so she said, "You must be very smart."

Without thinking, I said, "Not really, just lucky I guess."

Then a bell went off in my head!!

A little voice in my mind shrieked, "You did it again! You just put yourself down again!"

It just snuck up on me. I wish I had caught myself before I opened my mouth. And just as I was thinking that, Chris saw my grade and complemented me on it.

This time I remembered, and I actually said, "I'm tickled pink. It looks like all my studying paid off."

Talk about being tickled pink!! I just accepted a compliment!!! My studying really is paying off!

Right then and there I bent my elbow. Chris had no idea what I was doing, he probably thought I was scratching my back or something.

George said if I want others to see the good in me, I can't keep pointing out my imperfections.

He made a good point. He said if you keep telling people that you're not so great, they're likely to believe you.

My homework tonight is to write:
I ONLY SAY THINGS ABOUT MYSELF I'D WANT OTHERS TO SAY ABOUT ME.

Dear Diary,

I have been watching my words all day and I can see why people have been getting upset with me.

Right now, I'm upset with me too.

It never crossed my mind before that maybe I couldn't accept a compliment.

I never even heard compliments before.

I've always heard everything as insults.

Weird, huh?

This definitely feels better though.

That's why I'm trying so hard to learn this stuff.

George figured out a way to get something on my like list.

He said that since I like my hair sometimes, I should focus on it, until I can put it on my like list.

He wants me to become friends with my hair.

"How do I do that?" I asked.

"Talk to your hair", he said.

Talk to my hair?

That's what he said, I swear.

Every night when nobody is around, I'm supposed to stare at my hair in the mirror and talk to it.

I'm supposed to thank my hair for being on my head and looking so pretty. When I'm going to sleep at night, George said I should picture myself with my hair looking beautiful.

He wants me to keep doing this until I like my hair so much that my opinion is the only one that matters to me.

He said that when I really like my hair, there will finally be something I really like about myself and I will feel good about it even if somebody comes right out and says they don't like it.

Yeah right.

This I can't even imagine.

It's like saying that if people liked themselves enough, nothing anyone said would hurt their feelings.

Come on now.

Do you think that's even possible???

It really would be cool though, wouldn't it???

Dear Diary,

I had a talk with my hair today.

Are you believing this?

I thanked it for being beautiful, shiny, bouncy and soft.

My hair said, "Are you talking to me????"

"Yes you." I answered. "And now that you know how gorgeous you are, I expect you to act that way.

Again, my hair replied, "Are you sure you're talking to the right head of hair????"

"I'm certain," I said. "Now get with the program!"

Of course then I realized I don't even know a program and thought it just might be a good idea to get one.

When Mother said she was going to her hair stylist, I asked if I could go too.

I went....and Wow! I really do have pretty hair!

The stylist said the secret was products, products, products.

Well I don't know if it was the products or the talk, but my hair never looked this good before.

Even Rodney noticed.

He looked at me and then did a double-take.

All I can say is Wow.

If that's what happens when I talk to my hair, I may just start talking to every other part of me too.

Dear Diary,

Have you noticed that I hadn't been mentioning Rodney much lately?

That's because I gave up on him.

After that embarrassing day in science class, I just wrote him off.

Until yesterday that is, when he did the double-take.

He smiled at me again today. I could see in his eyes that he liked my hair.

He noticed me and he noticed my hair.

I felt like doing cartwheels!

I didn't know a little old hairdo could make such a difference.

ooo-gotta go now.

Mother said she likes seeing me interested in taking caring of myself so we're going to the store to buy those amazing products, products, products.

She's letting me get everything the stylist used on me. I'm so excited.

Do you hear what I'm saying D???

I can have beautiful hair every single day now!!!

George had gymnastics today, so he didn't have time to give me a lesson.

It doesn't matter though. I feel so good that I don't think I have a problem in the world.

Dear Diary,

What a beau-ti-ful day.

I feel so great that I've been grinning all day.

I told George I don't need any more lessons.

He said, "Don't kid yourself."

What is that supposed to mean?

I am doing well and boys are noticing me now.

Rodney was absent from school, but some other boys and a few girls said they loved my hair today.

What a success!

I'm going to wear it the same way again tomorrow and just hope Rodney will be there.

Dear Diary,

What a lousy day.

It's too cold.

I have too much homework.

I don't feel like doing my chores...

AND Rodney didn't even look my way.

My hair looked just as good as it did yesterday, but he didn't even seem to notice.

I kept looking at him, but he kept looking at Mallie Huey.

And she wasn't even having a great hair day.

I am so frustrated. I could just cry.

What should I do now????

Maybe it's time for the next lesson from George.

But then again, maybe not.

I sure don't need to hear George say ,"I told you so."

I need to find somebody besides George who can cheer me up without George ever knowing I was down.

oh.

That's what you're supposed to do Diary.

Remember?

I'll just go back and read what I've told you, and it will be like you telling me what I need to hear right now.

Dear Diary,

Everybody should have a book like you for a friend.

You made me realize that most of my days have been good ones lately, so one lousy day is really no big deal.

It was fun to see how much better I am now at liking myself, too.

Remember when I wrote to you that I was talking to my hair so that I'd learn to like something about myself? Well, do you know what reading that made me realize?

When Rodney seemed to notice my hair, I started thinking I was fixing it for him, instead of for me.

I forgot how important it was for me to like my hair and I went back to my old way of thinking that it was more important for Rodney to like it.

But now I remember....

So let me bend my arm and give myself credit for doing something right.

I just have to keep reminding myself that I can have a good day whether Rodney notices me or not.

I have to remember that it's more important how I feel about myself than how anybody else feels about me.

Dear Diary,

Rodney was flirting with Mallie again, but I didn't let it get to my attitude.

Actually, I'm feeling pretty good today. I even told George that although I don't really need his lessons anymore, I want more anyway.

That actually made him smile. He said it's more fun to improve yourself because you want to rather than because you think you have to.

He wants me to pick one thing on my dislike list and figure out how to get it over to my like list.

That doesn't make sense. The things on my list are who I am. I can't change who I am.

"wrong", was George's response.

He says people can improve anything they want to.

In fact, George said I should change the title of my dislike list to my 'want to improve' list.

Oh. That does make a difference!

I told him that bend-the-arm thing was working too.

I realized that I don't do everything wrong and now I pay more attention to what I do right than what I do wrong.

"Woo-Hoo! Any day now you may actually like yourself," he teased. "And that's a good thing for me too, since I have to live with you.

"People who don't like themselves are pretty annoying to be around."

Okay then. That's not me anymore.

Besides this self-improvement stuff is actually kind of fun.

Dear Diary,

Since shyness was number one on ~~my dislike list~~ my need-to-improve list, I've chosen to work on it first.

Wendy says that my shyness keeps the boys away. She says I should never ignore people that I don't know very well because it makes them feel rejected.

She says other people don't know that I'm shy. They think I don't like them or that I'm stuck up or something.

I don't want them thinking that, so today I made a special effort to be especially friendly and at least smile at everybody, even if I didn't talk to them.

You know, it really wasn't such a hard thing to do after all.

Not that I made any new friends....but still, it felt good.

Tomorrow we have square dancing. I know it's a dorky old-fashioned dance, but what if I can't even do that?

Everybody keeps changing partners and I'll have to dance with boys I don't even know very well.

I'm just not comfortable interacting with people I don't know well.

Oh duh.

That's what shy is, isn't it?

Well tomorrow is a new day and I have promised myself I will join the square dancing and no one will even know I'm shy.

I'll fake it till I make it.

Dear Diary,

Well I found out why so many kids like our square dancing class......It really is a lot of fun!

You get to hold hands with one boy and then another and then another and you're supposed to sort of flirt with them all.

No wonder a lot of the girls got asked out.... including me!!

Kevin asked Jennifer if he could walk her home after school. Rodney asked Mallie to go roller skating on Saturday and Brian even told Stephanie he loved her.

When Jeff asked me to go to the Carnival with him and his family, I thought he was just trying to join the crowd.

I mean, I've known Jeff for a long, long time and he has never even paid me any attention before.

At first I thought he just asked me because it seemed like all the boys were asking girls out today and maybe he just didn't want to feel left out or something.

But then I realized what a super self-put-down that was and I changed my thinking.

After all, I am a nice person, I do some things right and I do have pretty hair. Why shouldn't he want to ask me out?

It's a good thing I promised myself I wouldn't let shyness get in the way of my fun anymore.

Do you realize what I'm telling you D??????????

I'VE JUST BEEN ASKED OUT ON MY FIRST DATE!!!!!!

Woopidee Doo!!!!!

Dear Diary,

Woopidee Doo??? Did I say that? Do I even talk like that?

Maybe I'm trying to get over being shy a little too fast.

Maybe I really am shy and it's nothing I can get over. I'm really scared!

I've been thing about my date a whole lot and I just might chicken out. I mean, this is my first date, you know.

Maybe I'm not ready for it.

What if I goof up?

What if Jeff doesn't have a good time?

What if he tells all the kids at school that he had a lousy time with me?

I mean, if a boy doesn't like you and never get to go out with him, that's one thing....but if you go out with him and then he doesn't like you....ouch...........that could really hurt.

You know there really is an advantage to not having any self-love.

If you don't like yourself, then nobody else will like you. If nobody likes you, they don't ask you out. If they don't ask you out, you don't have to take any chances on being embarrassed.

Then again, if nobody likes you, you don't have any fun.

Okay. I'm done spazzing out.

I can do this.

Dear Diary,

I told Wendy that Jeff asked me out. She was all excited for me. We're getting to be best friends again.

I told Wendy that I was excited, too, but I wished I was going out with Rodney instead of Jeff. (even though Jeff is cuter than Rodney)

Then that brilliant friend of mine said something that can only be described as 'truly intelligent'.

"You chose Rodney as your boyfriend before. If you CHOSE to CHOOSE Jeff as your boyfriend now, his smiles would mean just as much to you as Rodney's.

You have a choice to make"

That is downright intelligent.

So what I'm hearing is that my real choice is if I should go out with Jeff and enjoy it the most I can, or go out with Jeff and keep thinking about Rodney so neither of Jeff or I will have a good time.

Well Diary, which one do you think I'm choosing?

You know how intelligent I am.

Not how intelligent I used to be........I mean how intelligent I am now.

Dear Diary,

Mother took me shopping tonight after dinner. She said I could chose a new outfit to wear on my date.

I picked out a grey shirt with black and red writing on it shirt and a new pair of red skinny jeans.

I topped it off with a silver chain and a silver bracelet.

Mother wasn't really crazy about my outfit, she had picked out a sun dress with a little jacket. She thought I should choose something more feminine.

Then I reminded her that she had said that I could choose a new outfit. Also, I told her, it's more important how I FEEL in my new clothes than how everybody else thinks I look in them.

"Well, ex-cu-u-u-se me," Mother teased. I didn't know you were so sure of yourself."

"Neither did I", I answered and we both laughed.

So this is what it feels like to be in charge of yourself. I have been searching so hard for the person in charge of himself and that person is turning out to be me.

Yea Me!

By the way D, I did get the clothes I really wanted and I can't wait to wear them.

Dear Diary,
   Only one more day of waiting.
   Tomorrow is finally my big date.
   Carnival here we come!

   I would tell you more D, but nothing else seems very
important right now.

Dear Diary,

I am writing to you very early today for 2 reasons.

One is that I hope that I have such a big day that I am too tired to write when I get home.

The other is that Jeff and his family won't be here to pick me up for another 30 minutes and if I don't do something to pass the time, I'll just go crazy.

I have been dressed for 2 hours already and I think I've brushed my hair and fluffed it at least 200 times.

I am ready, ready, ready and I'm tired of waiting, waiting, waiting.

Guess what - I see their car!!!

Dear Diary,

It may take me days to tell you all about my late great first date.

Then again, it may not.

Some things feel so good that you don't even want to try to explain them. I think this may be one of those things.

I'll tell you something funny that happened though... Jeff and his brother made a bet to see which of them was the biggest chicken.

They both tried to go on every ride there and outdo each other. Jeff wanted me to go on every ride with him.

I was determined not to be the biggest chicken in the bunch so I went along with the bet.

Wouldn't you know somebody yelled, "Last one to the Ferris wheel is a loser."

My heart sank. I would much rather be a loser than ride on that Ferris wheel again.

I froze. I didn't know what to do.

Suddenly, Jeff grabbed my hand and started running in that direction. I guess he made my decision for me, but I made a major decision for myself at the same time.......

I decided not to let anybody know how heights scare me. (Or, as George would say, how I scare myself in high places.)

I kept repeating over and over in my mind, I NO LONGER CHOOSE TO BE SCARED IN HIGH PLACES.

I still screamed the whole time, but I was laughing at the same time, so Jeff had no idea how close I was to panic.

Jeff kept laughing because I was laughing. It was hilarious. We had such a great time!

At least I wasn't as scared as I was the first time I went on a Ferris wheel.

Part of my brain kept screaming, "You might fly off this thing!!" And the other part kept telling me I was strapped into the seat and nobody ever fell off this thing and stuff like that.

All that aggravation I went through with George paid off after all ...and I guess you could say that George was even right....

All I had to do to make the super-scared feelings stop was to get part of me to decide not to be scared any more.

I have to admit that I never would have believed it if I hadn't experienced it myself.

Dear Diary,

I waited all morning for Jeff to turn around so I could smile at him.

He finally looked at me at the end of second period.

Then I smiled at him...kind of a flirty smile.

The guess what?

He WINKED at me!!!!

It must be my hair.

It must be my dress.

"NO," said my self-confidence,

"It must be me."

Dear Diary,
   I'm happy.
   My hair looks terrific.
   George is fun to be around.
   I am already finished with my homework.
   And Jeff likes me
   and I like me
   all at the same time.

   Can it get any better than this?

Dear Diary,

Today we had a very unusual assembly and took a very unusual test. It's not the kind of test you study for.

This one was to find out what we already know.

The program was called A Self-Empowerment Series and it was run by a motivational speaker named Ms. Bright . She called her test The Intelligence Test.

I thought George would love it so I copied it for him.

You just mark yes or no.

Ms. Bright said subject tests could show how much students know about a particular subject, but true intelligence is measured by how much you know about using your mind to get the kind of life you want.

Do you think that could be true?

Then why don't schools have a class in this kind of intelligence?

Well, I guess some schools do.

That's what she's here for.

THE INTELLIGENCE TEST

1. Do you realize that it's hard to like your life when you don't like yourself? ☐☐

2. Do you realize that people don't have to think you're perfect for them to like you? ☐☐

3. Do you realize that it's impossible to be perfect because people can't agree on what perfect is? ☐☐

4. Do you know that you must believe you're lovable before you can really feel loved by another person? ☐☐

5. Do you understand that doing something bad isn't the same as being something bad? ☐☐

6. Do you have a habit of thinking that everything is your fault? ☐☐

7. Do you realize that your subconscious translates guilt feelings into 'punish-me' signals? ☐☐

8. Do you realize that when you change your thinking, it feels like the whole world has changed? ☐☐

9. Do you know that you can learn to change anything about yourself you want changed? ☐☐

10. Do you know that if you can see your part in creating a situation, it's easier to believe you can have a part in fixing it? ☐☐

11. Did you know that you can be happy at any time by deciding your happiness is the most important thing to you? ☐☐

12. Do you know that you'll discover new parts of ☐☐ yourself when you try new things?

13. Did you know that Einstein proved that we don't all share the same reality, that what seems right to each person depends on his perspective?   Yes □ No □

14. Did you know that your perspective depends on your opinions about that subject? □ □

15. Can you tell if an opinion is really your own or if you have taken on another's without seeing if that's actually what you think? □ □

16. Did you know that although you can't change things that have happened, you can change the way you look them? □ □

17. Did you know that if you can see things differently, even your feelings will change? □ □

18. Do you understand how your thinking creates your experience of reality? □ □

19. Did you know that finding something to be grateful for makes you feel happier? □ □

20. Did you realize that complaining actually makes you feel worse? □ □

21. Do you know that when you gossip, it makes people worry what you'll say about them? □ □

22. Are you aware that only opinion that counts in your life is your own? □ □

23. Did you have any idea that liking yourself was so important? □ □

Dear Diary,

Guess what???

I think I've discovered George's whole secret!!!

I thought there was something curiously similar to things on the intelligence test and the things George says so I gave the test to him.

Bingo!

George started grinning and said, "I guess this means you met Ms. Bright."

I knew it. I knew it.

"So you weren't born knowing this stuff?" I asked.

"Pff. Nobody is.

"You have to learn everything somewhere."

He said it like I should have known that.

I didn't.

"Well what were you like before?" I questioned.

"Let's just say that when I took the intelligence test, I thought it was some kind of joke. I kept waiting for the punch line.

I had never heard anyone talk about things like that before. I really couldn't picture anybody feeling like had a choice about how they felt."

"George!", I yelled, "Are you trying to tell me that you weren't born happy?? Then how come you've been so mean to me all this time, acting like I was a dummy because I didn't know what you did?"

George grinned. "The truth is, we'll never know for sure if I talked to you differently, but we do know for sure that you hear things differently now.

"Think about it. If I said, "You changed your hair," and

you didn't have any confidence, you would think that meant I didn't like your hair.

"If I said that to you now, you'd think it meant I do like your hair.

"My point is that I never said whether I like it or not.

"Whatever a person thinks is true or is afraid might be true, determines how they interpret what they hear.

"Imagine I tell you that you should change your hair color because it doesn't look good blue. You know your hair isn't blue, you wouldn't take it as an insult because you'd know it wasn't true.

"That means whenever you feel insulted, you had to be criticizing or doubting yourself first."

He makes it sound like it doesn't matter what somebody says, it just matters how I take it.

George is still always a step ahead of me, but we've actually become the best of friends. Although I do wish I knew if it was me that has changed or George.

Do you remember when I said that a great birthday present would be to get George to stop bugging me?

Well do you realize I got just that?

Do you think that means I could have some of the other things on my 'not within reason' list, too?

Dear Diary,

I have been thinking some more about the intelligence test and George. He said that his whole class took the test two years ago, but I just realized that I haven't met many people that think like George.

If so many kids have taken this test, why don't more kids have peace of mind?

And why aren't there more kids that like themselves?

And why doesn't everyone in George's class control his feelings?

And why isn't everyone who ever took the test happy most of the time?

And if Ms. Bright has given the intelligence test to so many different classes, why does all this knowledge seem so unfamiliar?

My mind is spinning. I have got to figure all this out.

In the meantime. I've got to go to the mirror and get on with my lessons.

Today I am talking to my face. I need to get my nose, my mouth and my eyes to work together a little better so that I can love (or at least like) my face.

And I've got to get done with this little exercise fast so I'll have time to talk to Jeff when he calls.

Dear Diary,

Jeff asked me to go skating with him and a bunch of kids Sunday afternoon.

It should be great fun.

Actually it should be greatly funny. I've never tried to skate before, but when Jeff asked me to go, I didn't have to think about it, I just said yes.

It seems that ever since I decided that being shy wasn't fun, the shyness has just been melting away.

It makes me think that once I really make up my mind to stop being a certain way, it's really fairly easy to change.

Jeff has been walking me home from school nearly every day since our date.

I've really been enjoying his company and I haven't been doing anything special to get him to like me.

Funny, isn't it?

Now that I've stopped trying so hard to get people to like me, more people do - and one in particular, seems to like me very much.

Maybe that's the secret to having friends - of course it could also have something to do with liking myself more now.

Nah. That can't be it.

Dear Diary,

Mother came home in the best mood tonight and said she had been thinking about George and me.

Her friend at work was saying how her kids drive her crazy by arguing so much.

It was then, Mother said, that she realized she hadn't heard us fighting in quite a while.

She told me that even though she hasn't said anything, she's noticed how I've changed. She said she likes the way I'm not overly sensitive anymore and that I don't go around complaining like I used to.

She said, on the whole, I am just more fun to be around than I ever was.

Wow. That was a nice surprise.

And I guess that answers my question about whether it was George or me that has changed.

I really don't feel like I'm doing anything different than usual though.

Than means number 8 on the intelligence test must be right -

Do you realize that when you change your thinking, it feels like the whole world has changed?

Dear Diary,

I still look in the mirror and talk to my face everyday.

Now I understand why George likes to have his alone time. There are some things I just wouldn't do if anyone else was around. Talking to myself is one of them.

Everyday I talk to my face and say , "Skin you have given me a lot of trouble in the past, but now I understand why. I didn't appreciate you before.

"But now I see that you would just love to co-operate with me and become beautiful. Look how gorgeous hair has become. Now you should be able to believe anything is possible.

"I mean really skin, are you going to let hair show you up? You can do anything she can do!

"Eyes, I now give you permission to express yourselves fully. Since you reflect what I am thinking you should be sparkling all the time now.

"Nose, it's time I made peace with you. I have called you big and ugly too long. I know you're not going to get any smaller or change your shape, so it's time I started accepting you the way you are and stopped thinking that you need to be any different.

"Face, we are now the best of friends and now you know what I expect of you. "You wouldn't like to let a good friend down now, would you?"

I still think that talking to my body is very weird, but this kind of weird has made the biggest difference in my confidence. And we all know that confidence is ver-ry attractive.

Dear Diary,

Stephanie is driving me crazy!

We have a geography test tomorrow and she's worrying herself silly.

Every time I quizzed her on the capitals of the world and she couldn't remember an answer, she'd say something ridiculous like, "I just hate myself. I'm so stupid."

I tried to calm her down. She just whined, "You don't understand. I should be able to remember this stuff. I studied it. I must be stupid."

I tried to convince her that stressing out was only making it worse.

I reminded her that she needs to like herself even if she's not perfect.

I told her that the only thing that's stupid is criticizing herself, but that didn't exactly gain me any points either.

Finally, I just gave up.

I guess she has to be free to be miserable if she wants to.

It doesn't make sense to me though. She acts as if she never took the intelligence test.

She still acts like she doesn't have a choice how she feels about things.

Maybe she just forgot.

Or maybe the Universe wanted me to know what it's like to deal with someone who is criticizing herself constantly.

Dear Diary,

We already took our geography test today , but Stephanie is still stressing out. We haven't gotten our grades yet, but she's worried about getting a B.

She thinks if she doesn't get an A on everything it will make her a failure or something.

I reminded her about question 11 on the intelligence test-

> Did you know that you can be happy at any time by deciding your happiness is the most important thing to you?

Stephanie worries so much about her grades that she makes herself miserable.

She's come pretty close to making me miserable, too.

I mean I can understand studying hard and wanting to do your best, but once you've taken the test it's a little late to worry about it.

With my new attitude, I look at it this way - If the way you think about your grades keeps you from feeling happy, then even if you get an A, you just failed.

Listen to me - I believe I'm beginning to sound downright intelligent.

Dear Diary,

We got our grades on our geography tests today. Jeff got an A, and I was so proud of myself. I got a B.

Stephanie got a B, too, but she wasn't exactly proud of herself. She got all dramatic on me and I just wanted to shoot her.

Come on. What's the deal? You study. You take a test and whatever grade you made, well - it is what is.

Then you get to say anything you want to yourself about the grade you made.

According to the intelligence test, it wouldn't be the brightest move to choose to insult yourself now would it? I mean what good is that going to do?

You know, my class isn't any different than George's.

All the kids in my class took the intelligence test, but not too many of them have changed the way they look at things. Maybe it takes more effort than they want to put into it.

Maybe they thought it was a joke of some kind. I mean the stupidity test was going around not too long ago and that WAS a joke - although some of the kids took that one seriously.

Remember the stupidity test?

You ask someone if they know what the first signs of mental illness are?

You say," the second sign is hair on your knuckles."

When they start looking at their knuckles, you tell them, "and the first sign is looking for it."

Dear Diary,

George took me by surprise.

He said he didn't know why I spent so much time working on myself. He said everybody knows you're ugly and your mother dresses you funny.

I was shocked. I was speechless. I just stared at him in disbelief.

I got a bit defensive and asked, "What's your problem?"

About that time, he starts talking like a computer voice. "This is a test. This is only a test."

"By the way..... you passed."

"Oh really? How did I pass?" I asked.

"Let me put it this way - if you had thought that you were the one with the problem, you would have failed the test."

I didn't want to tell him that although my words passed the test .....my thoughts did not.

Dear Diary,

Ms. Bright substituted again today.

She told us that since this was supposed to be math class, she was going to teach us some new math.

Then she drew a diagram on the board that looked like this:

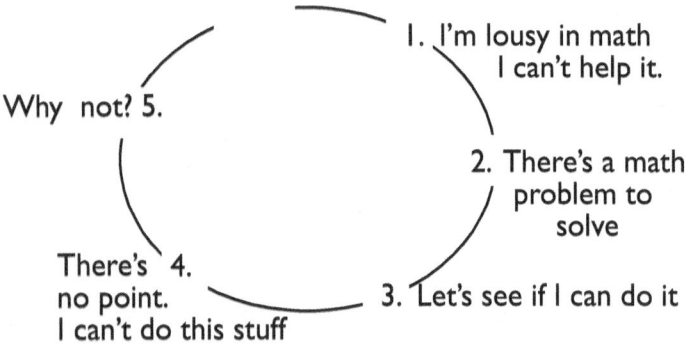

Ms. Bright called this the I'M CIRCLE. She said this is how our thinking keeps us running in circles.

When we think we're a certain way, like lousy at math or something, everything seems to prove us right, but it's really just our own belief that's keeping us in the circle.

"The trick," she said, "is to question what we believe about ourselves.

"If you can change your mind," she said, "then your I'M CIRCLES change automatically. You see, whatever you believe to be true about yourself, your mind always tries to prove that you're right."

Hearing that, it makes me want to say a few good things about myself and let my mind prove THEM to be right.

Ms. Bright drew another I'm Circle to show us how it works.

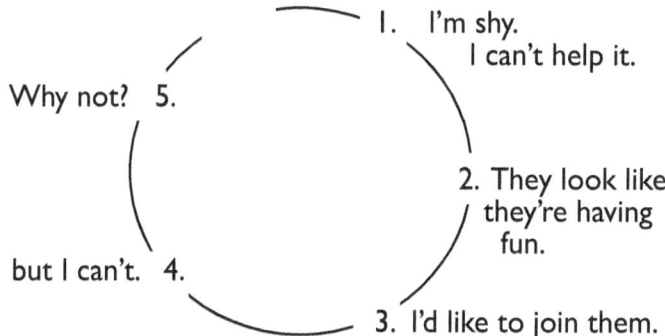

1. I'm shy.
   I can't help it.

2. They look like they're having fun.

3. I'd like to join them.

but I can't. 4.

Why not? 5.

As long as this character keeps believing he's shy, he'll just keep repeating his shy behavior and his experiences will tell him he can't change it.

He has a choice though. He can have a new thought. One that says he could try being social instead of shy just to see what it feels like.

This way he can break the circle and eventually create a new one for himself.

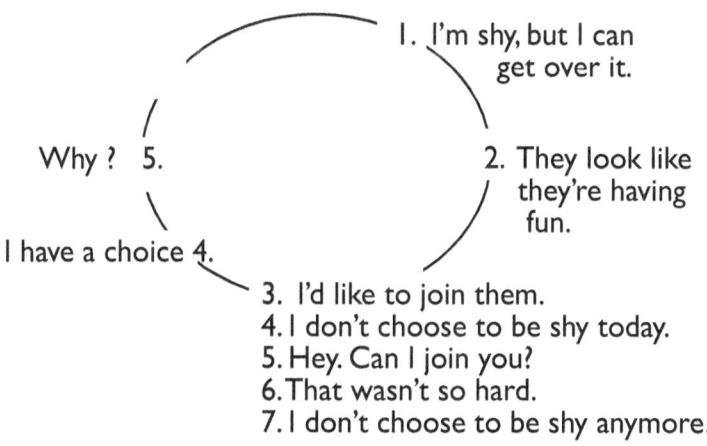

1. I'm shy, but I can get over it.

2. They look like they're having fun.

3. I'd like to join them.
4. I don't choose to be shy today.
5. Hey. Can I join you?
6. That wasn't so hard.
7. I don't choose to be shy anymore.

Why ? 5.

I have a choice 4.

Somebody asked Ms. Bright how she could call that math.

Her answer -"Well, that's how our choices ADD up, isn't it?"

Everybody made faces and went, "o-o-o-o-h-h".

I sure do like her.

I wish she was a regular teacher.

She gave us some homework for the weekend.

She wants us to make a list of the "I'ms" we use so we can discover any I'm Circles we've trapped ourselves in.

Hey! Did you hear what I just said???

Ms. Bright gave us homework.

I hope that means she'll be back again Monday.

Dear Diary,

Stephanie came over today and we did our homework together.

We both thought of a bunch of I'ms for our lists. I wrote down:

1. I'm poor in geography
2. I'm a lousy cook
3 I'm uncoordinated
4. I'm too tall
5. I'm not musical
6. I'm forgetful
7. I'm weak

Stephanie was surprised at some of the I'ms that I wrote down.

She tried to give me a hard time by saying, "I thought you were the one that learned to like herself so much. How come you have so many I'ms?"

I don't know where it came from, but the words just came out of my mouth, "Well I guess this just proves that I've learned to like myself even though I know I'm not perfect."

That shut her up.

Actually that was a pretty good answer, wasn't it?

It sounded like something George would say.

Dear Diary,

    Sunday. Sunday. Beautiful Sunday.

    Jeff and I spent the day riding bikes in the park and listening to music. Mother even invited him to stay for dinner.

    The only I'm circle I've been working on today goes something like this:

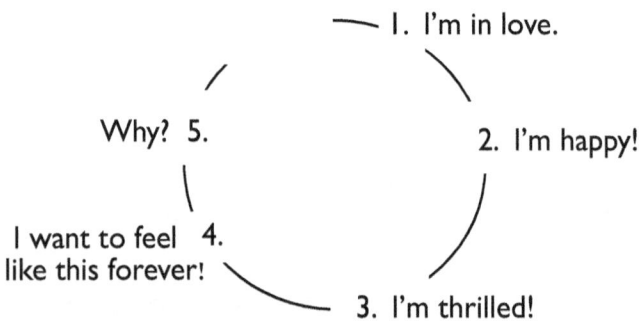

Dear Diary,

Great day! Ms. Bright was our "math "teacher again. We all teased her and asked her what the "math" lesson for the day would be.

She smiled like she does and said that we were going to work on subtraction.

"That is, we'll be working on subtracting the I'm Circles we don't want from our lives."

Of course we had to do the "o-o-o-o-h-h-h" thing, but we were really looking forward to it.

Ms. Bright gave us a few new ways to look at our I'ms so we could make the choice to change them, or should I say "subtract" them.

She said that all of our I'ms are just habits.

Some we may have just picked up from listening to someone else, some we started because at the time they made sense and then we never really thought about them again.

"Our I'm lists give us a reason to think about our habits and our beliefs." She said. "You don't even have to decide to change a habit, but at least decide to stop criticizing yourself for it."

What a concept. I love it. That DOES sound intelligent.

Then she said we should only try to change one "I'm" at a time. When you hear yourself say a negative I'm statement, just pause and correct it by saying, "Well, I used to be that way, but not so much anymore."

Today I realized that when I say I'm lousy at something, I tell myself I won't like it. Then, I never even try it - like dancing.

That makes no sense though. Nobody gets good at anything unless they try it, learn it and then practice it.

Okay. I have my new line- If somebody asks if I'm good at something I'll say, "I don't know if I'd be good at that or not. I haven't really practiced that yet."

And I'm adopting a new motto for myself....

Anything worth doing
is worth doing poorly
until I've done it enough
to do it well.

Dear Diary,

Unfortunately, our classes returned to normal today. Too bad. I really like that self-help stuff.

It has really helped me change how I see myself and my life. I even told Jeff that I'm going to cross 'I'm a lousy dancer' off my list because of our square dancing class.

It turned out to be so much fun and I really think with a few lessons and enough practice I could probably be a good dancer.

Jeff's thinks we should help each other get rid of one I'm circle at a time. He's working on his spelling.

I said there was one I couldn't work on because there's nothing I can do about it.

That's my I'm too tall circle.

Jeff grinned, "You say that like tall is a bad thing."

We both laughed. We're getting good at this, I think.

"Really?" he asked, "What are you too tall for?"

I don't know. I tried to think of something so I said, "I'm too tall for a short boy."

"I'm not short," Jeff said.

No, but that's the best I could do. I didn't have another answer.

Anyway we started talking about Jeff's spelling.

He said it was always easier to say he was bad at spelling than to have to study it. I'm afraid that's what it's going to take for him to get better at spelling.

You know, I'm really lucky to have a boyfriend who wants to improve himself and is even willing to put out the effort to do it.

Dear Diary,

A friend of my mother's stopped by last night. When we were introduced, she said. "You are so tall. You ought to be a model."

Me? A model???? I was flattered.

Then I thought, I'll bet she just said that to be nice to my mother....... I didn't say that though.

You'd be proud of me for what I did say.

Heck, I'm proud of me. I smiled and said, "Thank You."

"Oh yes. I've come a long way," I said to myself as I patted myself on the back.

I called Jeff and told him what my mother's had said. I thought he'd get a laugh out of her compliment.

He didn't laugh though. He said, "Actually you might not be tall enough to be a model."

The he started laughing and said, "That's perfect. You went from being too tall to not tall enough in a matter of seconds. I think you just found a way to break your 'I'm too tall' circle."

When I said there was nothing I could do about being too tall, I didn't realize I could change my perspective.
    duh.

Dear Diary,

Jeff got a C on his spelling test.

That may sound lousy to most people, but he was thrilled. He usually gets D's.

His I'm Circle has officially been broken.

It started out as "I'm lousy at spelling."

Now it's "I'm at least average when I study."

That's a start.

But I think he's determined to improve even more since his Dad told him that to get a good job as an engineer, he has to be able to communicate well and that includes spelling.

Jeff may want to be an engineer someday so now he has reason to improve.

He said he knows he can do anything once he makes up his mind to do it.

Well you know I believe in that.

It's my turn to pick another I'm Circle. I picked the one that says I'm uncoordinated.

Wish me luck. I have a feeling I'm going to need it on this one.

Dear Diary,

I asked my family if they thought I was uncoordinated.

They started laughing and said when I was a baby they used to say I gave real meaning to word 'toddler'.

I remember George would always say things like "You can't walk and chew gum at the same time."

I told them I didn't want to be uncoordinated anymore.

They laughed again.

Dad said, "I don't want to discourage you, but coordination is something you are born with. You either have it or you don't".

Ouch.

If that's how he talks when he doesn't want to discourage me, I'd hate to hear what he'd say when he does.

I've been thinking about that conversation all afternoon. If the intelligence test means what I think it means, then I DO get to choose.

I don't have to be born with every good trait.

My family said they thought I was cute when I was awkward. Maybe I kept being that way because I liked when they thought I was cute.

And George always has his one-liners to tease me.

Maybe I never took it as teasing and I just assumed he meant it. And maybe once I believed it was true, I started acting like it was true.

I think the opposite of uncoordinated would be graceful.

I wonder who teaches how to become graceful? Because now I've got to know.

Dear Diary,

I told Stephanie my new goal of becoming graceful.

She's the one who always calls me twinkle toes, but I've never been sure whether she meant that as an insult or a compliment.

So I asked her.

"It means you walk like you have two left feet. So I guess it was an insult," she answered.

"Too late!" I yelled. "I took it as a compliment. I thought it meant I was light on my feet."

She just rolled her eyes.

I don't know why Ms. Bright said you should talk to the people who gave you the labels and tell them that you have decided to change.

To hear their opinions is positively depressing.

It's a good thing I remember #22 on the intelligence test. The only opinion that counts in your life is your own.

Before, this kind of feedback would have just made me give up. Before, I would have been hurt and angry that a friend would think so little of me.

Now I just tell myself that I am the only one in charge of my life.

I tell myself that Stephanie is only treating me the way I taught her to treat me.

I tell myself that doing something is not the same as being something.

I tell myself that when I learn more I'll do more.

Then I tell myself that since I want to be happy every minute, I have to believe all the things I've been telling myself.

Dear Diary,

George cut an ad out of the paper for me. It was an ad from a local dancing school that was offering several kinds of lessons.

I told George, thanks anyway, but that I've decided not to take dance lessons right now. Maybe in a few months.

He understood exactly how I was feeling.

He said it was my choice and he just wanted to make sure that I knew that.

How silly. Of course I know it's my choice.

He said, "I was just afraid that maybe you were letting other people's opinions make that choice for you."

Good old George! He did understand how I was feeling.

Give me that ad!

That's what I'll use my blank check for. That would really be a meaningful birthday present!

Dear Diary,

Jeff and I were talking about our brothers today and Jeff said I was so lucky to have George for a brother. He thinks George is funny and he loves talking to him.

I never thought I would agree, but George has been like a real friend lately. He even talked Mother into calling to enroll me in that dance class.

Now that's something he wouldn't have done a few months ago - just another example of how George has changed. He says he hasn't changed, but how he treats me has definitely changed.

George says it's because I changed. He says I bring out a different side of him now. He even teases me differently.

He used to make jokes 'about' me. Now he makes jokes 'with' me. It's like he cares about my feelings now.

He still teases me, but he makes sure that I laugh, too.

I used to tell him, "George. It's only funny when we BOTH laugh", but he never listened.

He has a new thing though. When he teases me and I'm not sure if he means it, he laughs and says, "I'm so funny."

I usually say something like, "Thanks for telling me," and then we both laugh.

I only wish everybody was so thoughtful.

Dear Diary,

Guess what?

Dance class starts tomorrow. I'm nervous and excited at the same time.

I didn't tell Stephanie yet. I'm going to wait until I learn some steps so she won't be able to tell me that I won't be able to learn it.

I don't know what she's going through, but she sure has been critical of everybody lately.

She started gossiping about Sonya, the new girl that just moved here. I was afraid she'd make everybody dislike the girl before they even got to know her, so I interrupted her and said, "I'm surprised to hear you talk like that about her. She says such nice things about you."

That took Stephanie by surprise and it shut her up, too. I acted annoyed and quickly walked away before she could ask what Sonya had said.

Which was a smart move, especially because I never heard Sonya say anything.

When I hear somebody talking behind someone's else's back, I have this awful feeling that they're going to talk about me behind my back, too.

It just makes me want to avoid that person. I think if people realized how it made others want to avoid them, they wouldn't want to gossip anymore.

It's not a very endearing quality for sure.

Dear Diary,
Oh wow!
Dance class was amazing.
I don't even care if I'm good at it or not .
It's just so-o-o-o much FUN!!!!
I just wish it was more than once a week.
I'm so glad I tried it!
Look what I would have missed.

Dear Diary,

I know I said I wasn't going to tell Stephanie, but I was about to pop. I was still excited today and I just wanted to tell everybody how great it was.

Stephanie actually said she wanted to take the lessons, too.

"Except," she said, "I'm not very good at that kind of stuff. I'd probably make a fool of myself."

Can you believe it?

I thought she just felt that way about me.

I told her just to take it for fun and not need to be great at it or anything.

I told her the only way to break the kind of I'm Circle that she's in, is to face her fears head on. And we both know the only way to get over the fear of looking bad dancing, is to learn to dance half way decently.

I hope she has the nerve to try.

Jeff said my happy attitude is giving him the courage to keep working on his Circles.

It makes me feel good to know that I inspire people, but to hear that I inspired them just by doing something that makes me happy .... is pretty darn cool.

Dear Diary,

I wish Stephanie wasn't going to join the dance class. I want to get away from her. She's getting on my nerves.

She always finds something to worry about and whatever it is that day, she makes sure that it dominates our conversation.

I used to get caught up in it. I spent a whole lot of energy trying to help her and solve her many problems and try to make her feel better.

I don't want to do it anymore.

I've been learning how to think differently and take responsibility for my thoughts. It's time for her to do the same.

I know we all have freedom of choice, but if she doesn't start choosing differently, I won't be spending much time with her anymore.

Her worry habit has to be broken.

Seriously now. I can't think of even one time when worrying accomplished anything.

Well that's not totally true.

When Stephanie worries, she does create a lot of drama and that drama has been getting her a lot of attention and all that attention does makes her feel important and special.

From now on, if she wants attention from me, it will have to be because she's talking about something besides a problem-something worth talking about - like boys, or boys or did I say boys??

Dear Diary,

I feel terrible.

I got so wound up about Stephanie's worry thing that I opened my mouth and complained about her to Mallie and Wendy.

And then it got back to Stephanie and now she's mad. She yelled at me, "It says right on the intelligence test that you should avoid gossiping if you want to be intelligent. I thought you were such a big fan of the test."

No.no.no.no.no. She's not going there.

I'm not going to sit here and hate myself because I told some of our friends that her constant drama is getting on my nerves.

It's true that I asked them if it was getting on their nerves too, but that's not the same as gossiping. I think they only told her what I said because they agreed and didn't have the guts to tell her that they thought the same thing.

Change of plans. I'm done feeling guilty, even if somebody does count that as gossiping.

I remember when Wendy told me that if I kept criticizing myself that she wouldn't hang out with me anymore, so now it's my turn to tell Stephanie she has to stop all the drama with the worrying about things that will probably never happen.

I mean really, look how much my life has improved since I stopped criticizing myself so much. Wendy actually did me a favor. Well now it's my turn to do Stephanie a favor.

Dear Diary,

Jeff and I went to the movies and guess who we ran into?

Mallie and Rodney!

I guess they're going out now.

Mallie asked if we wanted to sit with them and we did. It was great.

Rodney flirted with me when no one was looking. I sort of flirted back.

Not that I would trade Jeff in or anything, but after feeling rejected by Rodney, his flirting was flattering.

We went for pizza afterwards and had a great time. Rodney really is a nice guy. We had a lot of fun.

They said they'd like to double date again.

You can count me in.

Dear Diary,

Remember when I said no one was looking when Rodney and I flirted?

Um. I was wrong.

Jeff called tonight and said if I'd rather be dating Rodney he would walk away.

He said to consider us broken up so that I have the freedom to pursue Rodney again without feeling guilty.

OMG. It was only a little harmless flirting.

Jeff said he wasn't trying to say that what I did was bad, he just wanted me to know that there are consequences to our actions.

He said that if I really thought I wasn't crossing any lines, I would have flirted right in front of him and Mallie, instead of waiting until we had both walked away.

That was actually a good argument. Rodney and I both knew enough to wait until we were alone, but then I told myself there was nothing wrong with innocent flirting.

Obviously, part of me did know better. I guess I can use that as a test from now on. If I wouldn't do it if people were watching, then I shouldn't do it at all.

I really blew it now - and things were going so well.

I do feel guilty.

But not for crushing on Rodney. I really wasn't. I was just enjoying his attention.

Ugh. I want to shoot myself.

What should I do??

I need to talk to George.   NOW!

Dear Diary,

Good old George came through for me again!

I was stressing and crying and hurting from feeling so guilty.

When George said I was making myself miserable for no good reason, I admit I came unglued.

I thought he hadn't been listening to me. So I told him again, "I screwed up and Jeff broke up with me! That seems like a good reason to me!"

George stopped my tirade. "I heard you, but I dont hear you saying what you're going to do about it"

He says that when you feel guilty, you make yourself miserable by wishing you had control over the past.

You don't.

In the present moment, you have to accept what is and figure out what you can do about it.

"Talk about solutions. Not about problems!"

George said while I'm upset, I just keep talking about the problem with everyone except the one I should be talking to and he's the only one that can help solve it.

George told me to call Jeff and admit I made a poor judgement call and let him know I'll never make that mistake again.

The most fascinating part to me, was when George explained that when we feel guilty about something, we believe we deserve to be punished. Subconsciously, he says, people pick up on that belief and think they are supposed to punish you.

Holy Moly. Do you think that could be true????

I really want to make this right with Jeff, so before I call him I need to forgive myself and make sure I stop feeling guilty.

I surely don't want Jeff to think he needs to punish me.

Dear Diary,

I called Jeff and apologized. I admitted to him that I made a poor choice, but I also made it clear that it wasn't my fault that Rodney flirted in the first place.

Even though it was embarrassing, I went ahead and admitted why I flirted back.

I told Jeff that before I dated him, I thought Rodney was the best, but now I know that for me, the best is when a wonderful guy also treats you like a best friend.

I promised not to do anything like that again and Jeff said then we could be a couple again.

We went to the mall for something to do. I started playing with a box of cards called ANSWERS.

You're supposed to ask a question and pull a card to get your answer.

I couldn't think of a question, so I just asked, "What do I need to hear?" and then pulled a card. It said:

> There is a price to be paid
> when we sacrifice what we want most
> for what we want at the moment

So accurate it's a little spooky. Jeff said that card said it better than he could have, so he bought me the box. How sweet!

Every time I play with it now, I'll think of two things:
1. That I'd better learn from my mistake
    2. Jeff is a sweetheart!

Dear Diary,

I told George that I was glad he had told me about guilt communicating, 'I deserve to be punished'. Luckily, I forgave myself before I talked to Jeff and then he forgave me, too.

Then George explained how we let others control us by making us feel guilty about things.

No sooner had we said that than he got an opportunity to illustrate his point.

Mother yelled, "George will you go to the basement and bring up 10 folding chairs?"

George yelled back, "Okay. In a minute. I want to finish what I'm doing first."

Mother then began her usual routine which goes something like this: "Never mind. I'll do it myself. Even though I have a bad back. You just sit there and enjoy yourself."

Everything was sounding rather typical and I was expecting George to worry about Mother hurting her back. Then he usually jumps up and hurries to do whatever it is.

Here is where things changed from the usual.

George winked at me and whispered, "Does that sound like a guilt trip to you?"

I smiled.

Then he yelled. "Okay Mother, if that's what you want to do I won't try to talk you out of it."

Then we heard her footsteps coming out way.

We had to hold our breath so we wouldn't giggle.

She yelled, "What's so important that you can't come right now?"

84

George started smirking. "Are you saying that I am so lame that I couldn't possibly be doing anything even remotely important enough to want to finish it first?"

Mother raised one eyebrow like she does and answered, "Oh come on now. What could you possibly be doing up here?"

"That's cold," George said. "We do things that are important to us. Surely that counts for something."

Mother just answered, "Whatever. Just get the chairs."

"Not a problem. It's first on my list after I finish what I was doing."

Mother did the hairy eyebrow thing again.

"It'll only be a minute," George added.

"One minute," she said and left the room.

I'm not sure who won that one, but at least George didn't feel like he was manipulated by a guilt trip and he got to state that his thoughts matter, too.

George says if he stays on his toes and catches himself whenever she tries making him feel guilty, he'll teach her that guilt doesn't work on him anymore and then he can teach her what will work.

Dear Diary,

Stephanie called after school and said she wanted to come over. She said she missed our friendship and thought we should talk.

When she came over, I decided to get out my box of ANSWERS I told her to just ask for a card that's perfect for now.

The card she picked said:

> Don't worry about tomorrow.
> Hoping it gets here fast,
> 'cause you'll waste all your present
> Like you wasted all your past.

I cracked up.

She said she didn't think it fit anything.

So I handed her a piece of paper and asked her to make a list of everything she's worrying about.

When she finished, I told her to put a check mark by the things that might get better because she worries about them.

Of course she didn't check anything off.

She said it was embarrassing to realize what I'd been talking about.

It reminded me of when I couldn't see why it would bother anybody that I didn't like myself.

We gave each other a hug and made up.

Now we both understand why intelligent people don't choose to spend their time worrying.

Dear Diary,

My algebra teacher called my parents today and asked them to come in and talk about my 'problem'.

Normally that would have given me reason to worry, but knowing that sickening feeling in the pit of my stomach wouldn't change the outcome anyway, I decided to just relax and take it as it comes.

I know that somehow this will all work out just fine. (Not that I have any clue how, but that's what you have to tell yourself when you don't want to worry.)

My father, however, is more comfortable when I get all worried. I think it's one of those annoying parent things.

You know, like they always want you to be fearless and confident - except when it comes to them.

He says I have a flip attitude - what ever that is.

He says I'm acting like I don't care.

First of all, I have no clue why I might be in trouble.

Secondly, I'm very disappointed in my Dad's attitude. He hasn't even gone to the conference yet, but he's already sure that I've done something horribly wrong.

Well sorry Dad, but in my book you have just done something horribly wrong. If somebody said something bad about my Dad, I'd defend him no matter what. Clearly that doesn't work the other way around.

It amazes me that this teacher thinks I've done something horrible enough to call my parents about, but doesn't see fit to talk to me about it first.

Tell me again why we want to grow up to be adults.

Dear Diary,

I'm glad to know that not worrying was the choice I made. I have gone two whole days without worrying over this ridiculous conference which finally took place today.

I only wish ANGER was a choice, because I am ANGRY, Mad, Furious, Upset, Irritated, Infuriated, in a Rage and even Resentful.

Furthermore, the only color I can see is RED!

You just will not believe what the point of that stupid conference was!

Miss Abda says I've changed. She says my stubborn streak is getting out of hand. She says I refuse to do my homework and she wants my parents to punish me.

I told her the first time I get less than a 97 on a test, I'll start doing homework. I thought we were here to learn. I learned it. What else matters?

What is her problem? You know there's something else bothering her. Nobody can really argue with that.

Oh, sorry. Did I say Nobody????

As crazy as it sounds, my Dad agrees with the teacher. Mostly because she is the teacher and therefore she can do no wrong.

He said I have to stop being so stubborn. He said that I am in school to learn and I should do EVERYTHING the teacher tells me to do whether it makes sense to me or not.

I expected Mother to understand. I explained to her that I always get the highest grade in the class without doing homework.

Miss Abda doesn't grade homework and she doesn't give points for doing it or not doing it. It makes no sense to use my precious time learning what I already know. There are lots of kids in the class that barely pass. She should be calling my parents to praise me!

I closed with, "Some teachers forget you're in school to learn. If you ace every test, I think that says you must have learned what they want you to."

I guess my closing argument wasn't as great as I thought it was because she came back with," You ARE stubborn. Why can't you just do the homework?"

That's when I started seeing RED!

No matter what you do that you think is good, someone will always find something wrong with it.

Well, guess what. I admit I'm stubborn and I'm not going to change. I am very happy with my algebra grades and I refuse to stress just because I have an unreasonable teacher.

What can they do to me anyway??? Hang me??

Mad as I was though, I still knew better than to argue with my parents.

That's one thing they just can't handle.

I just told them I was really surprised they felt that way and then I tried REALLY hard to keep my big mouth shut.

By the time we got home and they let me go to my room, I was so mad I just wanted to break something!

I didn't, of course.

Everything in my room is mine and why would I

punish myself for something that I don't think is my fault in the first place.

It's SO-O-O-O hard to be a kid!!!!

There doesn't seem to be any acceptable way to handle my anger.

When Mother and Dad get mad, they yell and scream a lot and sometimes they even slam a door or leave the house.

Do you know what would happen to me if I did any of those things??? My parents seem to think that I should never get mad.

After all, I'm only a kid, they say. You don't have any real problems, they say. You don't even know what real problems are.

"Get real", I think - not that I'm going to say that, but it is what I think.

Finally, I pulled a card out of my box of ANSWERS. The card said:

Would you rather be right
or happy?

What a ridiculous question.

I'd rather be both.

Dear Diary,

Dad asked to see my algebra homework when I left for school this morning.

When I said I didn't have any, he came unglued.

He said that trick wasn't going to work on him. He thought I was being unnecessarily stubborn and then he said I was grounded for a week.

"Time to worry?" I asked myself.

"No", I answered. "Worry doesn't help any situation."

Stay cool, I told myself. Hang loose. Maybe he had a bad day at the office and he's just taking it out on me.

I did think about calling Dad a few choice names at this point though, but then I decided I wasn't ready to die, so I didn't say a word.

I'm sure I rolled my eyes, but I turned my back first so he wouldn't see it.

Dear Diary,

What a lame art class we had today.

My art teacher drew a tree.

Then she passed out colored chalk and told us to draw a tree.

What she didn't tell us though, was how she was going to grade our papers.

As it turned out, she didn't seem to notice how well we used the chalk or how good our colors were, how we used our imaginations or even how pretty the picture turned out.

She graded them by how well we copied her tree!

That's not art!!!!

She shouldn't have told us to draw A tree, she should have told us to draw HER tree.

I was not among the ones that figured that out ahead of time.

I mean, how was I supposed to know??

I thought this was art class!

Just look outside. All trees don't look alike.

I was so proud of my tree, too. I drew lots of purple flowers and almost no leaves. It was beautiful.

At least to me.

Miss Finch looked at it and wrinkled her nose. "Trees don't grow like that," she said.

Then I wrote on it, "Artsy Tree."

She gave me a C anyway.

Jeff's tree looked just like hers, so he got an A.

Jeff said that just because they call this Creative Art, it doesn't mean they want you to be creative.

And I should know this, how?

Instead of getting super mad though or letting my feelings be hurt, I remembered that how I felt was MY choice.

I added a few letters to the C she wrote on my art work.

My paper now says CREATIVE.

I happen to like my picture.

I refuse to give anyone permission to ruin my day.

And that's the good side of stubborn!

Dear Diary,
   I have to admit I'm bored and slightly depressed.
   Mostly because...I'm still grounded
   Jeff asked me to go to the lake with his family this
weekend, but I'll still be grounded.

   I didn't know a week could be so

L

O

N

G

Dear Diary,

This has been a very trying day, but to tell you about all my little upsets of this afternoon would just make me remember everything I that I would rather forget.

Let's just say that everything that could possibly go wrong, went wrong.

I'm trying to do everything Ms. Bright taught us though, so I keep thinking about how I want things to be instead of how they appear to be.

I've been trying everything to keep from being thoroughly depressed.

1. I said to myself, "Self, just choose to be happy anyway." That really hasn't worked though.

2. I read my Intelligence Test twice to remind myself of how I choose to feel, but my wagon is still draggin'.

3. I tried getting busy doing something, but I just couldn't seem to make myself.

4. Finally I fell down on the bed and imagined being at the lake with Jeff. I saw myself laughing and having a great time.

Fortunately, that has been working.

It was tricky at first, but I've got this system figured out now.

It's kind of like the time Ms. Bright brought out a clock and said, "Now sit quiet for a minute, and think of anything you like, but don't think about this clock.

"Don't look at it. Don't wonder what time it is. Don't wonder how much time has gone by, just don't think about this clock at all."

Finally, we started complaining and saying, "If you don't want us to think about the clock, you're going to have to stop talking about it!"

"Exactly," she said with a smile.

"When there's something that doesn't please you, stop talking about it!"

"It's the same with moods and depressing thoughts. It's impossible to NOT think about them, but if you look in another direction and concentrate your thoughts on something totally different, you automatically stop thinking about those depressing thoughts."

So I remembered that and I've been having fun with Jeff in my mind, which is almost as good as being with him in person.

Well, it's better than anything else I can think of now though, so that's how I'm spending the rest of my day.

Dear Diary,

A-a-a-a-h! I want to scream!!!!!!

Remember the day Mother said she was so pleased with the way I've changed?

Funny. She doesn't seem to remember that today.

She ran into Miss Finch at her women's club and remarked about the way Miss Finch marked my art work 'Creative'.

Miss Finch of course told her a different story.

So now Mother thinks that I was intentionally trying to cover up the truth.

It seems Mother and Miss Finch had a discussion about how different I seem lately - and they didn't mean that in a good way.

They both said they couldn't put their finger on it, other than to say it was an attitude change.

Excuse me, but wasn't that what the Self-Empowerment Series was all about?

I don't argue with George anymore.

I don't pout anymore.

I still don't talk back, even when I think my parents are wrong. My grades are decent. I've been happy. I've been doing my chores even when Mother isn't here to tell me to do them.

Do I need to walk on water now too?

They don't seem to be looking at all the things I'm doing right, just the couple things they think I'm doing wrong.

Dad threw his hands in the air and said, "I just don't know what to do with that girl."

Let's see now.

For starters he could be proud of my independent attitude.

He could realize how nice it is that I've learned to think with my own brain.

He could appreciate my self-assurance.

He could admire my self-esteem.

Or... he could just leave me a-lone.

He didn't think of those things though. He said I have an attitude problem and I was now on restriction until I fixed it.

You know what that means, don't you?

Adults are more confused than teenagers.

On one hand they want us to develop 'life skills' so we will be prepared for life and become successful in all that we do.

On the other hand, they don't think they should have to respect our brains and our input. They don't want to be questioned even when they don't know what they're talking about, or should I say, especially when they don't know what they're talking about.

They want us to develop skills and only use them with their permission - with other people, that they will never have to meet. They want us to know how to think for ourselves and make good decisions when we leave home, or do they?

I think some of them hope we'll be emotionally dependent on them forever so they can always feel needed and maybe even always feel smarter than we are.

I think some of them would rather see us fall flat on our faces so they can say I told you so.

I think some adults feel intimidated by younger people who might do something better than they can as though that would invalidate them or something.

I think some adults care more about their image than the happiness of their kids. I think some adults want kids just to do what they say whether the kids are happy or not.

I'm probably exaggerating - I'm so wound up. I'll shut up now.

Dear Diary,

I had to tell Jeff today that I'm not allowed to see him for a while and he didn't understand at all.

He thought I should do whatever it was my folks wanted me to do just so we could spend time together.

Of course he'd think that. He was willing to copy Miss Finch's tree and never discover what his tree would have looked like.

I have to admit I'm confused though.

To be completely honest, I don't even know what my parents want from me.

I have really been feeling great lately. I've been happy for the first time since I can remember and I can't see how I could be a problem to anyone.

The only attitude shift I'm aware of is what I call the new me. I used to feel helpless and thought my life was hopeless.

But now that I've experienced life knowing that my entire reality is my choice, I feel in control of my life and I love it.

It's not anything a person could give up once they know how great this feels.

I'm trying to imagine how that can feel so bad to the adults in my life when it feels so good to me.

I honestly don't get it, so I guess I'm grounded until college.

Dear Diary,

OMG! Could things get any worse???

I didn't get a chance to write to you last night, so I took my Diary to school and wrote yesterday's letter to you during science.

Now I admit that wasn't the best choice I could have made, but that's what I did.

Mr. Moss saw my Diary and decided to make an example of me. "And what have we here?" he asked.

I turned red. I told him it was my personal Diary.

"Well since you feel that class time is an appropriate time to work on your Diary, I think you should share it with the class. Stand up and read a few pages."

I gasped.

He couldn't be serious.

"Ms. Moss, I'm sorry, but this is my private book."

"You are the one who brought it to class," he insisted. "Now stand up and read!"

I froze. I absolutely froze. I just couldn't read this stuff out loud.

"Start reading NOW or you'll find yourself in the Principal's office."

I could see no choice. I quietly got my things together and headed for the door.

Then he really got mad! "Where do you think you're going?" he screamed.

"To the Principal's office." I answered, trying to show no emotion, but I was so upset that I almost broke out in tears.

Then he yelled something I had heard somewhere before. "I just don't know what to do with you!"

What's the deal anyway????

Why does everybody think they need to do something with me?

Why do all these adults feel so threatened just because they no longer worry me?

I can control me.

Nobody else has to.

Besides, Mr. Moss came up with the punishment and I agreed to it.

Why am I in trouble for that???

Dear Diary,

The straight-faced announcement I received at the dinner table was, "Your mother and I received a phone call today from your science teacher."

OMG.

What else can happen?

I was about to break inside. Tears came to my eyes. My stomach began to ache.

Suddenly a little voice inside my head said, "You can handle this. Just make the choice."

So I did.

I chose not to let the situation make me feel hopeless. I chose not to feel like a victim.

After all, I did something stupid and I am willing to accept the consequences.

I thought, "So they talked. So what? I mean really. Just what else can they do to me anyway???

I learned from my mistake. I guarantee you I would never even think about taking my Diary to school again. What good would it do to feel guilty about making that mistake?

And really, why would Mr. Moss even want to call my parents? They're not the ones that made the mistake.

That's how I thought anyway.

Then I started thinking about how parents think and I got a little nervous.

Parents don't seem to realize that kids have a brain of their own and make choices on their own.

They always seem to think if their kid makes a mistake it means they did something wrong.

I mean really.

I take my Diary to school and it becomes necessary to have another teacher talk to my parents.

I'd hate to see what would happen if I ever did anything that was really bad. It would probably become an international scandal.

Besides, anybody with a brain would know that Mr. Moss was wrong to expect me to read my personal diary to the whole class, but I don't see anybody calling his parents.

How could Mr. Moss think for one moment that my parents could teach me more about taking a diary to school than that embarrassing situation did?

Does he really think I'd risk going through that again???

As I thought all this through, I regained my composure. I was already on restriction. What else could they possibly do to me?

Outwardly, no one probably guessed all this was going on in my mind.

I didn't say a word.

And I didn't even roll my eyes.

Dear Diary,

Unfortunately, I got the answer to my question. Remember the one that goes something like this:

What else can they do to me anyway?

Well Mother admitted that she and Dad had to think really hard about that one. They said that none of the punishments they have imposed on me seem to affect me and they are tired of parent-teacher conferences, and they don't like being embarrassed by my behavior, so they have been racking their brains trying to think of something that will bother me enough.

Finally they realized the only thing they haven't taken away from me is my dance lessons.

What could I say?

Arguing is worthless at this point.

So is crying.

I feel like this time, they've gone too far.

The punishment is far greater than the crime. It's like prison with no rehabilitation program.

I know what they're trying to do. They want to break my spirit so it will be easier to control me.

They want to make me think it's too costly to think for myself or stand up for myself.

They want me to kiss up and act like only adults have any value, any brain or should get any respect.

It's not happening.

They can control my freedom, but I will not give up my mind. I just discovered it and I'm not giving it up.

Dear Diary,

It's you and me pal.

No more dance lessons.

No more going out with Jeff.

They even took my computer away.

And now I hear that when my friends call, Dad has been telling them I can't come to the phone.

I'd like to do something really awful just so they can see how good they've had it having a daughter like me.

Of course, I won't.

I'm smart enough to know it would hurt me more than it would hurt them and it wouldn't fix a thing.

You know through all their punishments and ranting and raving and complaining, they have never once told me exactly what they want from me.

They told me what they don't want, but I've yet to hear exactly what they do want.

They are so out of control and unreasonable, that it really does look like a helpless situation.

The only thing I could think to do was put in a prayer for some help.

They say ask and you shall receive.

Well I've asked.

And I'm more than ready to receive.

Dear Diary,

George has been strangely quiet lately and I was really starting to think he'd turned on me, too.

Thankfully, I was wrong. When he and I were home alone, we had a nice long talk.

He said he knew exactly what I was going through. He said his only advice was, "Don't let them break your spirit. You know how good you've been doing, but it takes a little while for people to adjust to the new you. Personally, I like the new you a lot. Be patient and be persistent."

He said that when he went through it, his class was hatching caterpillars that were about ready to turn into butterflies. He said he sort of related to them. But he felt like when he was ready to break out and fly, somebody tied a string around the cocoon and wouldn't let him try out his wings.

George said he felt his choice was clear. He could cave in and never know what it was like to float above the commotion of the world, or he could just be determined until he wore that string to a frazzle.

Then George told me something I didn't expect.

He said I shouldn't think less of people who aren't running to my rescue right now. Every butterfly has to find his own way out of the cocoon. People who jump in and help are demonstrating that they don't think you can do it.

Well he obviously thinks I can. Thank you George.

Dear Diary,

It's really hard to keep a good attitude and feel happy with my parents so unforgiving and all.

I'm seriously bored, too.

I asked George how much longer this whole process might take. He said it's anybody's guess.

"You're both waiting for the other to give in.

"The first one that does, is the one that has to change. If that's you, you'll be expected to go back to acting the way you used to before you learned so much. You'll be expected to care more about their feelings than your own.

"You'll be expected to act so scared and worried, that when adults want you to do something that you don't believe is good for you, you'll do it anyway.

"On the other hand, if they cave first, they'll have to change, but they don't even know what changes they'll have to make, so they're scared.

"Hang in there kid. No matter how long it takes. You can't afford to go backwards. Once you have self-respect, you really have to insist others respect you too. Even if they are your parents.

"I think you're winning so far. You haven't been rude or argumentative or even resistant. It's blowing their minds.

"They know you've got some new confidence that they can't touch. Why else would they say they don't know what to do with you?"

"Why do they say that?" I asked him.

"It means they don't know how to get to you.

"That's a good thing. Now you get to teach them how to interact with you if they want you to co-operate."

"I don't want to teach them anything. I just want them to be fair and care about my side of the story and how it makes me feel.

"I want them to sit down and discuss what's really bothering both of us and why.

"I want them to expect me to co-operate because I care about their feelings as much as my own and I don't like arguing.

"And I don't think they should over-react every time I make a mistake! I'm willing to learn from my mistakes and I'm willing to accept the consequences of my actions. And want that to be enough for them"

George just smiled.

"That's exactly what I meant."

oh.

Dear Diary,

The all-knowing, all-seeing adults in my life banded together at the regularly scheduled parent-teacher conference.

They decided that I hadn't done anything really bad, but that I refused to follow rules in general. They said I was getting a cocky attitude and it was the perfect time to nip this in the bud.

This goes against what even they, believe.

I looked up self-empowered in the dictionary. It says: 'deriving the strength to do something through one's own thoughts and based on the belief that one knows what is best for oneself.'

Hello. That's what I'm working on here.

Dad obviously doesn't get it. He said my restrictions would go on indefinitely. He said I could think of it as a life sentence and the only thing I can get a pardon for is good behavior.

I have a feeling this 'good behavior' he is talking about is a lot like the art teacher's tree.

I didn't say a word, especially since I learned this is what confuses him the most.

I did look him straight in the eye though and just hoped he could read my mind.

I think it's time we had a little parent-teenager conference to talk about being treated more like an adult.

Dear Diary,

I'm starting to understand why all the kids who go through the Self-Empowerment Series and take the Intelligence Test don't turn out like George.

Most kids would cave in the face of all this aggravation. If I didn't have George, I might cave too.

Mother and Dad are incredibly frustrated because they can't see that anything they've been doing has been affecting me.

It seems like if I acted depressed and worried and guilty, I'd get all my privileges back, but there's more at stake here than a few privileges.

I want them to have a whole new attitude now. I want to be appreciated and respected and I want my feelings to count as much as theirs.

I've grown up and now I want them to grow up too.

George says the trick is to keep smiling and singing no matter what they do to you. You have to let them know this is not the way to gain your co-operation.

The most amazing part of this whole mess is what has been happening inside me during this whole affair.

I have been working overtime on controlling my behavior and my thoughts with the power of my mind and making a supreme effort to sing when I feel like crying so that my parents and my teachers would never again think this was what they 'should do with me'.

Now I realize just how much control I have over myself, my feelings and my life.

I have really wowed myself this time.

It's hard to believe that girl that first wrote to you was really me.

And do you know what?

It just occurred to me I've accomplished one more thing.

I have discovered that anger really is a choice.

I've instinctively found ways of choosing not to express anger and in some cases not even to feel it.

Up until know I wasn't sure anger was a choice.

Speaking of choices, right now I choose to go to bed.

Good night!

Dear Diary,

When I got home from school today, I found a note from Mother taped to the refrigerator.

It said that besides all the chores I always have to do, she also wants me clean out the frig and wash it out, too, polish the outside of all the appliances, and do 2 loads of laundry.

Oh, yeah and it also had a P.S. -

It had better be done by 6:00.

Who does she think I am Cinderella?

I sank down to the floor and started to cry when George walked in the door.

"George," I whined. "She's got me this time. I can't keep up the good attitude anymore. Just look at this note."

That George, he's so beautiful... Do you know what he did????

He put on some music and helped me. We were working so fast and just singing at the top of our lungs.

We actually enjoyed ourselves.

Then George came up with the clincher.

He said once we finish all the things I was supposed to do, he said we should wash the floor, too.

He said to be sure I didn't let the cat out of the bag and tell anyone that he had helped me.

When Mother came home everything was sparkling and the music was off.

I saw her get out of her car and I could tell she was wound up and ready for a fight, but when she opened the door her jaw dropped. All she could say was, "wow". She was speechless.

I acted like it was no big deal and said something casual like, "Yeah, well, I started cleaning and just got carried away."

Then I went to my room.

The rest of the evening was unbelievably pleasant.

But like George says, "How could Mother stay mad after that?"

Dear Diary,

This is the loneliest Saturday of my life. I am the only one home today and I have to stay here. And I can't have any company.

I have to admit that I did sneak in a few phone calls, but that's the only communication I've had with the outside world.

It doesn't help that it's gray and rainy out too.

I've been trying to get myself to do something so I won't be so bored and depressed, but I just can't seem to get myself moving.

Day-dreaming about Jeff did the trick the last time, but this time I really feel low.

Even writing to you isn't helping. I think I'll see if I can find a good book to get lost in.

Want to hear something funny? I found a book on the shelf in the study that looked kind of interesting. I opened it in the middle and read: A sure cure for depression - Look in the mirror and force yourself to smile for 5 minutes.

I just tried it. It's a riot.

At first it was a real effort to smile, but then I started to feel so silly that I started giggling.

I guess that is a sure cure.

Dear Diary,

    Mother is coming home late tonight.

    George and Dad and I had to fix dinner for ourselves.

    I baked some potatoes, and fixed a salad. George grilled some hamburgers and Dad fried up some okra.

    We really had a great time working together and the meal was terrific, if I do say so myself.

    And I do.

    I know it softened Dad, too, because Jeff called and Dad even let me talk to him.

    My life sentence hasn't been repealed yet, but I can feel it coming.

    There just might be something to that line parents like to use. You know - the one they say when they punish you, "This hurts me just as much as it hurts you."

    "Then why do it?" I always think.

    I never believed it before, but I'm beginning to think they would love to find a way to justify taking away all these restrictions.

Dear Diary,

My life sentence has been repealed!

I don't really know why .... something about some book Mother started reading.

But that's not the important part!!!

I got ALL of my privileges back!!!!!!!!

The first thing I did was call Jeff and tell him I was coming over.

Then I went to the closet and took my computer back.

Oh, and it gets even better.

Mother said she's going to support my independent thinking from now on.

Of course, she also said, 'within reason', but that leaves the field wide open, now doesn't it?

Dear Diary,

I think happy days may be here again!

Mother says she has adopted a whole new outlook on things since she has been reading a book she borrowed from a friend.

She said the author has really made an impression on her and she wants me to know how much she appreciates me and the way I've handled all the stuff that's been going on around here.

"After reading this book, I believe I could have handled things better. And if I had known these things earlier, I would have, I assure you," she said.

Wow. I NEVER expected that.

What is this book she's reading? I love the author already. Imagine someone writing words that could actually get my mother to look at things differently.

Oh, yeah, and she said from now on we'll sit down and talk before she gets so upset.

She actually said that she respects me for being so willing to accept the consequences of my actions.

She even said that from now on she wants to be sure she's being fair to me and she can only do that when she knows how I feel.

Did you hear that D?

My mom actually cares how I feel!!!

What a book this must be that's she has found.

This is a day I'll remember for the rest of my life!

Dear Diary,

I feel so great you'd think I just won a gold medal or something!

The whole world feels happy!

It feels like a day we should celebrate so I called and ordered a pizza for delivery!

I ordered my favorite toppings with a cauliflower crust. George never heard of cauliflower crust, but I ordered it anyway.

George is celebrating my release like it was his!

I think he's happy that our mother suddenly feels like she's on our side.

Jeff is so delighted that we can spend time together again that he asked me to go steady and even asked me to wear his ring on a chain around my neck.

Mother is busy and has a new twinkle in her eyes. She is smiling to herself and I can tell what's on her mind.

She is picturing herself in control of her whole world and feeling rather proud of herself too.

When George tasted the pizza, he said it couldn't have been more appropriate. He said, "That's just proof! If cauliflower can become pizza, you my friend, can be anything you want."

But Dad, well...Dad is slightly shaken by all of this. He isn't sure what is going on in all of us. He's even trying to be stern and put a damper on things.

Only it isn't working.

That's okay.

This independent stuff can be catchy.

He's bound to catch it next.

Dear Diary,

Mother wouldn't stop raving again about how much good that book has done her.

She said she wished every parent would read it.
In fact, she said she wished every teenager would read it.

She said she just understands things so much better now.

I know something has changed.

She's happier and much nicer to us.

I told her I'd have to agree with her.

If that book could make such a difference in her life and in mine, I wish every parent would read it, too.

I mean I'm happy for her and all, but I don't understand why she keeps wanting to talk to me about it.

Anyway, Jeff and I are meeting a bunch of our friends at the ball game. Rodney's supposed to be there, but no problem.

I'm sure I won't even be tempted to flirt.

This is so great!!!

I have friends again!!!

Dear Diary,

    George had some friends over and one of them played his guitar for us.

    My favorite song was a short one by the Beatles called Blackbird.

    It just keeps playing over and over in my head since I heard it.

    Maybe because it's so appropriate.

Blackbird singing in the dead of night
Take these broken wings and learn to fly
All your life
You were only waiting for this moment to arise

Black bird singing in the dead of night
Take these sunken eyes and learn to see
all your life
you were only waiting for this moment to be free

Blackbird fly, Blackbird fly
Into the light of the dark black night.

    Of course, when it plays in my head, I'm singing butterfly instead of blackbird.

    It just fits, doesn't it?

Dear Diary,

What a fun day.

Jeff came over and helped us plan Dad's surprise party. He'll be 40 tomorrow.

Can you believe that? 4-0!

That's how he says it anyway. He says 40 is when you start to get old.

(Sounds like a choice to me.)

We laughed so hard when we were decorating his cake. It came out of the oven lopsided so we colored the icing green and wrote on it 'over the hill'.

Get it?

Everybody giggled about that one all afternoon.

That is, everybody but Dad.

When I asked him what he wanted for his birthday, he answered in his usual half-kidding way.

He said, "There's only three things I want and if I can't have them, I don't want anything.

"I want a 52 foot yacht, a million dollars and peace of mind."

He thought he was sounding funny, but I knew just how he was feeling.

And I know exactly what I'm going to get him!

Dear Diary,

I can't wait till Dad opens his present.

I don't think he has any idea that we're throwing him a party.

I think he's just expecting cake.

Mother even arranged for his boss to insist on a dinner meeting with him so it would be a surprise.

I spent the morning making his present. I like it.

I painted a skinny tree down the side of an ivory piece of paper then added little purple flowers (no leaves of course).

In my best handwriting I copied the Intelligence Test on it.

I folded the paper so it would fit in a tie box and on the top I wrote:

This box contains
one
genuine
do-it-yourself kit
for
peace of mind

D,

Mother walked in and started talking so quickly that I couldn't stop her.

She said something like, "Remember the book that helped me so much....the one I said every parent should read.....Well try not to freak..... but the friend I borrowed it from was you........and the book, well it's your Diary........I really think it's the best parenting book I've ever read.

"I really think you should publish it and let every parent read it!"

Wait.
What????